Erotic Tales

By K. Tarumi

Filidh Publishing

First Printing: 2020
ISBN 978-1-927848-50-0
Filidh Publishing
www.filidhbooks.com
Cover design by Danny Weeds.

Table of Contents

The Diary of Claire MacMillan

Volume 27: March 21 to August 15, 2012

Saturday, March 21

Today I had sex with John Baker, and it was horrible. I don't even like him, and he didn't know what he was doing. We were sitting in his mouldy Mustang after going to a lousy movie. He demanded that I take my pants off and move up and down on his manhood. He said if I didn't, he'd push me out of his car and leave me stranded on Mount Trojan. The whole thing was over in less than five minutes. "What if I get pregnant?" I asked him. "Don't worry about things that haven't happened yet," he snorted. Then he drove me all the way home without speaking a word. When he stopped in front of my home, I jumped out, slammed the passenger door shut, wiped away my tears, ran up our red-brick walkway and burst into our front door. Everyone was asleep, so I felt all alone, as usual.

Sunday, March 22

I woke up this morning with a sense of real relief—today, Mass was happening at 8 am. After quickly showering and eating breakfast, which included a coffee, a cheese croissant and a red crab apple, I drove to the Sacred Heart complex.

The beauty and majesty of our church are truly impressive. This morning the choir's rendition of *Jesu—Lamb of God* sent my soul into a state of pure peace. The flickering altar candles highlighted the sacredness of the service and the clouds of incense calmed me down. Father Jessop spoke of the most powerful antidote to worldly living—*pray without ceasing*. His mellow words were beseeching us to have our whole being stayed on God--from sunrise to sunset. What he was saying felt right to me as I sat there stuck in a morass of guilt.

On the way out, I stood in line for ten minutes just to speak with this holy man. When I finally reached him, I whispered,

"Can you give me the rite of confession this afternoon, Father—I really need it?"

"Why yes, of course," he answered. "Come back at 2 pm."

When I entered the church, there was an echo that rebounded off the clicking sound of my hard-heeled boots through the halls of that sacred space. As it turned out, Father Jessop and I were the only ones in the building at that time.

The door of the oak-panelled confessional creaked as I opened it. Inside, the air was warm and close, so I felt claustrophobic. The black curtain separating me from the padre moved slightly when he spoke—

"May the Lord be with you, Claire. Do you have any sins to confess today?"

"Yes, Father."

"What are they?"

"I had sexual intercourse on Saturday night with a man I don't even like."

"Why did you do that?"

"He forced me to do it."

"You're saying you were raped, then?"

"No, I let him do it."

"Why"

"Because I love sex, Father. I don't want to, but I do. Can I be forgiven?"

"Yes, our Lord forgives every sin confessed by a truly repentant heart. Have you had sex before Saturday night?"

"Yes, many times."

"How old are you?"

"Nineteen."

"Who else have you had sex with?"

"My uncle has taken me about fifteen times."

"How old is he?"

"Fifty-two."

"Is he married."

"No."

"Do you like having sex with him?"

"I love it, Father—but I don't want to. I hate myself for craving orgasms. He's a bully of a man and handles me roughly, but he satisfies all my sexual desires. And sir, I'm considering becoming a nun to cure this problem."

"Do you love God?"

"Yes, with my whole Being."

"Have you had sex with anyone else?"

"Just one other man—our next-door neighbour—he snuck into my bed on two occasions when my parents were in Mexico. I enjoyed him too."

"How old is he?"

"Forty-one."

"Is *he* married?"

"Yes—to my mother's best friend."

"Do you stimulate yourself to orgasm?"

"Yes, many times each week."

"You've been committing mortal sins which threaten to injure your soul *and* your relationship with God. This must cease immediately. Your penance is to stop any kind of sexual activity, including self-massage, intercourse, touching, kissing or any

contact with men, come to 7 am Mass every morning for a month and repeat two hundred *Hail Marys* for twenty days in a row."

"Thank you, Father," I told him, "I'll do these requirements wholeheartedly and with contrition."

"Can you help me become a nun?" I asked him.

"I can set up an appointment for you with Mother Mary-Cecile. She's the Superior at the Carmelite Convent in Orangeville."

"How long will it take before I get to see her?"

"Approximately one week--I'll email you when I've got the date finalized."

"Thank you, Father."

"May the Lord be with you, Claire—you can go now—but come back to confession in one week."

I felt so much relief having gotten my confession out that my guilt was easing as I left the church. It felt like a heavy burden just slid off my back, like a giant boulder rolling down a slope into the ocean.

<u>Sunday, March 29</u>

My second confessional went much better than the first. Father opened with his usual salutation:

"May the Lord be with you."

"And with you, Father," I whispered back.

"Have you been doing your penances?"

"Almost perfectly, Father."

"Where did you fall short?"

"On one occasion, I masturbated to orgasm."

"Did you have contact with any men?"

"A strange-looking man with a crinkly beard came up to me in Starbucks and offered to buy me a coffee, but I refused him and walked away abruptly."

"Anyone else?"

"A guy in a dirty cowboy hat asked if I needed help carrying my sister's wedding presents in the Walmart parking lot, but I said, 'No.' "

"You're a very shapely and beautiful young woman, Claire, and I can understand why men are attracted to you. But, you've done well to reject all of them this past week. Please double your *Hail Marys* to compensate for your one slip and make this coming week perfect."

"I will try, kind sir."

"I've arranged for you to meet Mother Superior on Tuesday of next week. She'll be waiting for you in her office at 7 am. Can you get there that early?"

"Yes, Father, if I can borrow my mother's Toyota Tercel."

"That's good. Let's convene next Sunday again at the same time."

"Yes, and thank you, Father."

"May the Lord bless and protect you, Claire."

Tuesday, April 7

It took me twenty-two minutes to drive the fifteen miles to Orangeville. Sea-green cacti lined the dusty dirt road into the Sisters of Carmel monastery as I drove along it. The sun was beating down, and it was hot, very hot.

I paused at the top of the steps before knocking on the double-oak entry doors. My palms were sweaty, and I felt flushed. When the doors eventually creaked open, I was staring at a young nun, immaculately dressed in full habit. Her black hood cascaded into a stiff, starched white vest attached to a grey dress with pleats reaching down to the ground.

"Hello—and welcome to Carmel—my name is Sister Eileen. How can I assist you?" she asked.

"I have an appointment with Mother Mary-Cecile at 2:30 pm today."

"Come in then and please have a seat in the lobby," she responded, pointing to a bench.

As soon as I sat down on that long, pine seat, I was overwhelmed by an exquisite painting of St. Teresa of Jesus. It stood twelve feet high directly across from me against white plaster walls. Teresa's right arm was holding a crucifix and her wide eyes gazed right over a black cape into my face. A white dove was flying above her in the design. The artist had clearly captured her charisma, grace and poise.

"Welcome to our Carmelite community, Claire. I'm Sister Mary-Cecile. Please join me in my office."

I sat down on the only available chair in front of her massive desk. Sister Mary-Cecile placed herself into a large, black-cushioned executive lounge chair with long arms. Behind her hung a large painting of Christ on the Cross, and I noticed the crown of thorns on His head and several droplets of bright red blood on His forehead.

It was an imposing situation for me. The Mother's chair sat on a slightly raised platform, so she was looking down when she spoke to me. She was an austere, stocky woman with wire granny-glasses sitting on her pointed nose. Her voice was unemotional, even harsh.

"I understand you want to become a Carmelite sister."

"Yes, I do, Mother."

"Do you realize that life here is rigorous and disciplined? We live an ascetic lifestyle that's dedicated to the commands of our saviour, Jesus."

"I think I do."

"Did you know we take vows of poverty and chastity?"

"Yes."

"I understand you have a problem with the sin of lust."

"Yes, Mother, I do—but I believe the religious life will cure it."

"Are you currently a devout Catholic?"

"Yes."

"How long have you been in the faith?"

"All nineteen years of my life."

"Well, Claire, I admire your intentions. But before you become a nun, you must try our lifestyle out, to see if you're suited to it."

"That sounds very wise, Mother."

"Each month, we hold a one week Retreat for young women. During that week, you'll live precisely as we do, and a nun-counsellor will be assigned to supervise you. There are practical and theoretical exams at the end of that Retreat. If you pass them, you'll be invited to become an Aspirant and enter our three month trial period. If you make it through that, you'll be eligible to apply for a one-year Postulancy, which further helps you discern if there's a vocation present. At the end of the Postulancy, if both the community and the candidate recognize an authentic call, admission to the Novitiate follows. The Novitiate is a two-year program that marks a true beginning into the life of a nun. It begins with the rite of initiation to a Religious Life. The candidate is given the habit of the Order, with the veil. The novice then enters more and more into the Carmelite way of life as she comes to know its demands--and experiences them.

"When does the next Retreat begin, Mother?"

"As it happens--next week—starting on Sunday. Would you be interested in participating?

"Yes, Mother, I would."

"That's fine then. I'll register you for the event. Please arrive at 7 pm on Saturday night. Sister Catherine will meet you in the lobby to tell you how to prepare."

"Thank you, Mother."

"Thank the Lord, Claire, not me. Bless you, and we'll see you on Saturday."

<u>Thursday, April 9</u>

At Mass this morning, I felt confident that attending the Retreat was the right decision for me. I threw myself wholeheartedly into the service—listening carefully to Father's homily, staring directly at all the burning candles and imbibing the Bread and Wine with spiritual relish. My lungs burst with enthusiasm when singing the hymns.

After the service, I stopped to speak with the priest.

"Father, I've decided to attend a week-long_Retreat at the convent starting this Saturday night. It's an introduction to living the Carmelite way."

"That's wonderful, Claire. You'll know if the religious life is for you when it's all over. Were you able to get a week off work?"

"Yes, Father, as you know, I'm the manager of Ryan's Christian Bookstore, so all I had to do was get someone to cover for me."

"That's good—I think you'll learn a great deal on this initial religious journey."

"I think so too, Father. But now I won't be able to attend confession with you on Sunday, as agreed."

"I understand, and that's fine. We'll resume confession on the Sunday *after* Retreat.

"Just make sure you keep up your penances and may the Lord guide and protect you until we meet again."

"Thank you, Father."

Two things bothered me about Father Jessop today. First, he'd told Mother Superior that I had a problem with lust. It was my understanding that everything said in confession was strictly confidential. Second, I noticed again today that he has a habit of staring directly at my breasts in an inappropriate way. Perhaps that's partly my fault for wearing a frock that reveals my ample cleavage, but surely a man of God is above staring right down my dress.

Sunday, April 12

When I showed up at the convent doors on Saturday night, the concierge was waiting for me on the cobblestone entranceway.

"Welcome to the Retreat," stated Sister Eileen. Come in and wait right here in the lobby. We have one other registrant joining us who I'm expecting at any moment."

Shortly after I sat down beside the painting of St. Teresa, another young woman could be seen standing in the open doorway.

"Are you here for the Retreat?" queried Sister Eileen.

"Yes, I am," she replied.

"You're Virginia Lincoln, then."

"Yes."

Virginia was a tall, attractive indigenous woman with large black eyes and long, jet-black hair. She had a certain poise about her but was dressed in a shabby way. Her jeans had holes in both kneecaps, and her denim vest was soiled with dark grease spots.

"Please follow me, girls, and I'll show you to your room."

"Will we be rooming together? I asked.

"Yes, you will," responded our guide.

Sister Eileen led us to a small but immaculately clean bedroom on the third floor. It had two single beds, a small desk and one chair. Sitting on the desk was a lamp with no shade, its single drawer containing a black Gideon Bible.

"You'll be called to rise at 5 am in the morning. Please put these white habits on when you get up, enter the hall and follow the other sisters to a small chapel one floor down. Once you're seated, there'll be a fifteen-minute period of complete silence as we prepare for Mass. At 5:30, you'll both join us in our choir stations for Lauds—our morning song praise of God. Then we'll move to the main chapel where the Lord will satisfy our spiritual hunger by giving us His Body, Blood, Soul and Divinity in Holy Communion. Once the service is over, I'll direct you to the next activity. Please remember at all times that our purpose is to *pray without ceasing* and *praise God*. Good evening."

"Thank you and good night, Sister," I said, as she closed our door and walked away.

"Are you going to become a nun, Virginia?"

"Yes, I do believe I am."

"Why?"

"All the members of my family are devout Catholics, and my parents want me to live the religious life."

"How old are you now?"

"I'll be eighteen tomorrow."

"Do you have a boyfriend?"

"No—I'm a lesbian with no interest in any kind of intimate relationship. Do you have a boyfriend?"

"No, but I'm an active heterosexual."

"Well, I'm going to say my prayers now and go to bed, Claire. We have to get up very early."

"Yes, after I go to the bathroom, I'll be going to sleep, too," I replied.

There was only one bathroom on our floor, and it was a communal one. It had two showers, four toilets and three sinks. There were about twenty lockers, some available for us to store our toiletries and personal items.

Monday, April 13

Before I fell asleep, Virginia got up and moved to the window, opening the translucent curtain that covered it. She stood there completely naked with a full moon shining on her exquisitely beautiful body, lighting it up. Her skin was a deep brown colour—like hot chocolate—and her back was taut as she stretched to open the window's top section, standing on her tiptoes. Her dimensions were perfectly proportioned with wide shoulders, a thin waist and long, athletic legs. Her breasts were the size of ripe California grapefruits, punctuated with long, dark-brown nipples. The last thing I saw before sleep overcame me was the most beautiful female body I'd ever seen. I slept soundly until 5 am when there was a loud knock on our door.

"Praise be to Jesus Christ and the Virgin Mary, His Mother. Come to prayer sisters, come to praise the Lord." These were the words Sister Eileen was chanting continued to chant as we both went out into the hall and followed several other nuns into a small chapel on the second floor.

I was still sleepy upon entering this space but soon woke up fully. It was an awesome place to be! Multi-coloured stained glass windows lined both sides of the enclave as the light began to stream in. A large replica of Michelangelo's *Pieta* dominated the front of the room. It was a statue of Jesus, with His head on the lap of his Mother, Mary, after the crucifixion. Beside them sat a long table covered with sea-green table cloths reaching the floor upon which sat twelve long, bright candles.

All of a sudden, the sisters knelt, and the room went completely silent. I was left to experience my own contemplations. The energy of twenty-two devout ascetics praying with intensity created a deep sense of peace within me.

At exactly 5:30 am, all the nuns sat back up on their benches and began to sing Lauds. Two hymns: the Benedictus and the Lord's Prayer—were all sung in a triple-- repeating pattern. This activity concluded with the chant—

"Glory to the Father, and to the Son, and to the Holy Spirit, as it was in the beginning, is now and will be forever."

After Lauds, we all stood up and moved in pairs—my partner being Virginia—downstairs to the main chapel for Holy

Communion. This was a full Sunday morning service with over thirty Catholics from the village attending. The sisters gathered in a special section at the front to quench their thirst for spiritual holiness by receiving the Body and Blood of Christ. That ceremony lasted for one hour, after which we all filed into the dining room for a breakfast of granola and fruit, supplemented by orange, herbal tea. Strangely, we had to eat in total silence and continue that silence as we carried our dishes into the kitchen for cleaning.

"Now it's time to praise the Lord through work, Claire and Virginia," whispered Sister Eileen. She directed us outside into a walled garden filled with four large glass greenhouses, rows upon rows of raised herb gardens and many stone shrines. "As you work, focus all your attention on your given task, working silently. If you wish to speak, address the One who's always with you--*inside your own being.* In two hours, we'll break for Sext, or mid-day prayer, to sanctify our labours by joining them to the passion of Christ."

My job was to scrub a massive statue of St. Teresa with a pail of soapy water and a wire brush. It was over eight feet tall, so I had to stretch high to reach her head. The labour was tiring because Teresa's stone figure had been left to get quite dirty. By dinner time, I was exhausted and extremely hungry. Again, we had to eat in silence, but I was too tired to talk anyway. After a meal of cold chicken breasts and a garden salad, we met with Sister Eileen to discuss our evening activity.

"Now, you'll meet your Spiritual Supervisor who'll be giving you classes in Theology throughout this Retreat. Her name is Sister Julianna, and her area of expertise includes the lives of the saints."

Virginia and I then found ourselves alone in a small under-furnished classroom, sitting at a long table, when Sister Julianna entered the room. She was an imposing character indeed. First of all, she was almost seven feet tall! Next, she was so much more alive looking than the other nuns. Her cheeks were red, her breaths deep and her flaming red hair flowed out of a black habit. Before she even spoke, I knew she was going to take a passionate interest in her subject.

"Welcome to Carmel, my girls. Tonight we're going to study the most interesting saint in the history of our church—St. Teresa of Avila. She was so holy she could levitate and emit a mystical light that would surround and protect her fellow sisters."

Tuesday, April 14

Virginia and I were so fatigued when we got back to our room that we stripped our habits off and jumped straight into bed. But, as I lay there tossing and turning, I felt a powerful urge to reach out to my roommate.

"I threw myself completely into our activities today, Ginny. It was very tiring but also purifying. I actually feel inspired by most of the things that happened. How about you?"

I didn't enjoy the gardening. Sister Eileen made me repot over a hundred tomato plants with my bare hands. Now I've got soil in the pores of my hands and under my nails."

"But did you like the church services, the singing and the prayers?"

"Yes, they were beautiful."

I was on the verge of sleep when Ginny's warm body nestled up against mine, and her right hand started massaging my stomach. Any kind of arousal was out of the question at that point—even though her touch felt heavenly—so I let myself go and fell into a deep sleep. When Sister Eileen knocked on our door the next morning, Virginia was back in her own bed.

"Did she sleep with me last night," I wondered, "Or was her forwardness just a crazy dream?"

Friday, April 17

The services, routines, singing, chanting, praying and working continued exactly the same way every day. There's something heroic and powerful about following the exact same patterns daily. It makes me feel protected from the chaos of the outside world. I feel I'm making progress and getting closer to God. All of the sisters are very helpful and patient, except for Mother Superior, who always seems condescending and critical.

The most inspiring part of the Retreat was Sister Julianna's instruction. With her red hair escaping from her habit when she taught and eyes that almost bulged out of her head, she takes us deeper and deeper into the life of St. Teresa. Our text was, *The Interior Castle*. The way she speaks about this book makes me feel she must have been one of St. Teresa's nuns in a former incarnation because she makes the work come alive.

St. Teresa teaches that there are many mansions inside our soul—each one offering guidance on how to proceed toward complete union with God. First, we have to learn how to be humble in our acts to allow grace to enter our lives. Then, by opening our hearts to Jesus, we can experience divine seduction.

The saint instructs us not to fear the aloneness each of us has to encounter in spiritual contemplation. According to her, if we pray with a pure heart and live in strict obedience to the will of God, the mysteries of life will slowly reveal themselves to us. I left Sister Julianna's classroom with tears in my eyes—determined to please God in all that I do.

I wasn't dreaming that Virginia came into my bed. She was now unashamedly sleeping with me every night. There was no sexual stimulation, but I enjoyed the warmth of her body next to mine.

"One of the reasons I want to become a nun is to cure my addiction to sex," I told her. "Right now, I'm engaged in several penances that Father Jessop gave me."

"Father Jessop gave you penances for a sex addiction?"

"Yes."

"That's crazy, Claire—he's got a huge sex addiction himself."

"How do you know that?"

"He's French kissed me on several occasions while he massaged my ass."

"Oh my Lord, are you sure?"

"I couldn't be more certain. But we won't have sex then, Claire—I just like you keeping me warm at night."

I wasn't sure how sinful this was, but I let her stay in my bed because my affection for her was growing. We talk whenever we can about the religious life and the teachings of St. Teresa. She, too, is inspired by Sister Julianna. But now, she's begun to confide in me. Her news about Father Jessop shocks and depresses me and makes my penances seem meaningless. Nevertheless, I keep doing them.

Saturday, April 18

Today was the last full day of the Retreat, and the scheduled events went as planned, just as they did every day. Virginia and I had each been given a copy of, *The Interior Castle*. We studied it intensely during any free times.

The Saturday class was given over to an exam on the teachings of St. Teresa. When we entered Sister Julianna's classroom, she was waiting for us with blank exam booklets. On the blackboard, she'd written two questions and told us to write our answers in the booklets—

1. What is humility?

2. What does it take to become an effective Carmelite Nun?

My answer to the first question stressed the need to openly admit my shortcomings and sins. I stated that there was nothing good in me and any positive qualities I might possess were God's work alone. Answering the second was more difficult. I described the essential themes of loving God first and foremost and obeying the Order's Rules--to the letter. Obedience to the Carmelite Edicts was how to protect ourselves from chaos, temptation and sin.

When the exam was over, I walked to the front of the room and hugged Sister Julianna.

"You've inspired me, Sister, and made me want to join this sisterhood more than anything else in the world."

"Claire, you've made good progress this week. I'll support your application for Aspirancy and recommend that you continue on the path of a religious life. Mother Superior will meet with you after Mass tomorrow to evaluate your Retreat and exam results. May God bless and protect you."

"Thank you, Sister—can I communicate with you while I'm away—in case I want to ask questions about *The Interior Castle*?"

"Yes, of course," she said and then gave me a small card with her contact information on it.

"Thank you so much," I replied.

Later that night, after I went to bed, Virginia, who'd also received encouragement from Sister Julianna, was telling me how much she wanted to become a nun when I fell asleep due to severe exhaustion. However, I woke up at 3 am with a start and noticed that my roommate was massaging my clitoris. I went to stop her but, by then, the pleasure was too great, and she was very proficient at the art of arousal. Suddenly, I had a massive orgasm and released a great deal of love juice onto Ginny's right leg. I remember thinking that a good orgasm was very much like the ecstasy of intense prayer among all the sisters—with only one difference. When the praying was over, I was full of peaceful, compassionate energy. However, the orgasm left me feeling drained, tired and ashamed.

"Virginia, that was amazing, but why did you do it? You know I'm trying to drop my sex addictions."

"You're too beautiful to resist, Claire," she replied with a deep sigh.

Sunday, April 19

Mass on Sunday, the final day of the Retreat, was spectacular. We sang our hymns with passion and chanted our prayers with authentic piety. Bishop E. M. Nelson gave a powerful sermon on how to avoid the ravages of sin. I was moved to tears by it.

After the service, I went directly into Mother Superior's office. I sat back down on that simple chair, facing her on the raised dais.

"You've made progress, Claire. We appreciated your efforts, especially during the work periods. Sister Julianna has nothing but high praise for you, and both her and Sister Eileen have given you a pass on your practical work."

"How did I do on the exam, Mother?" I asked.

"Your marks were very high. Are you interested in moving on to becoming an official Aspirant?"

"I most definitely am, Mother."

"Well, there's a three-month *Aspirancy Program* starting here in early September. Do you want me to register you?"

"Yes."

At that point, she took her glasses off and stared directly into my eyes, without blinking.

"It's not your nature to become a nun, Claire. You're subject to some very powerful addictions which we may not be able to heal."

"Yes, I'm a flawed woman, Mother—but I yearn for a life of purity and contemplation."

"I'll register you then, but be aware that we'll be watching you much closer during the three-month trial."

"Thank you, Mother, for your willingness to give *me*, a miserable sinner, the opportunity to become holy, gives me great hope and confidence."

"Intensify your devotion to Jesus over the next few weeks, Claire. We'll see you in September. May God bless you and keep you free from sin."

Friday, April 24

I was up early today to get ready for Mass. After saying my *Hail Mary's* and praying for thirty minutes, I gulped down a green apple and a black coffee and headed off to church. I was wearing a tight sweater with a short, plaited skirt and sandals with no socks. I didn't put panties on to protect my derriere, and there was no bra present under my thin purple sweater.

The hymns, chants and liturgy felt more real to me after a cloistered week. I'd become more attracted to all things holy, that's for sure. After the service, I stopped to talk to Father Jessop on the way out of the chapel.

"The Retreat was fabulous, Father."

"I'm so happy for you, Claire. Are you going to go back for more programs?"

"Yes--I've already registered for the three-month trial starting in September."

"That's wonderful," he exclaimed with enthusiasm.

"Can I come by your office today to tell you about some of the things that happened at the Retreat?"

"Yes, you can. Come by at 3:30 today, if you like."

"Excellent, Father, I'll see you then."

When I knocked on his door, he called out,

"Come in."

He was sitting in a soft, leather seat at his expansive executive desk and, as soon as he saw me, said,

"Oh, just a minute, there's a book here I want to give you."

He then walked over to the bookshelves and began looking through his collections. I then moved up beside him and leaned against his right arm, ever so slightly. He immediately put his hand on my butt and slowly began massaging it. I could see that he was flushed and breathing heavily. Once he realized I had no panties on, he lifted my skirt and continued rubbing my bare skin. It felt very nice, but I was not in the mood to extend the encounter as it was proceeding, so I turned toward him and looked directly into his pale, gray eyes as he turned towards me. All of a sudden, his lips were on mine, kissing me--and it was not just a customary, friendly kiss. He inserted his massive tongue right down my throat. Then he moved his right hand under my sweater and held onto my left breast firmly.

"What are you doing, Father?" I asked him.

"When you love someone, and your heart is pure, a little physical intimacy can be allowed," he replied sheepishly.

"But you told me this kind of activity was a mortal sin."

"It can be, Claire, depending on the motive of the sinner."

"Father, please stop touching me. I'm enjoying your advances, but this is inappropriate--and **you**, of all people, know I'm trying to overcome my sexual cravings."

At that point, the priest stopped feeling me up and walked back to his desk.

"I can't seem to find the book I was planning to give you, Claire. When I do get a hold of it, I'll make sure you get it."

"What book was it?"

"*The Way of Perfection*, which I believe is St. Teresa's finest work."

"Thank you, in advance, sir."

"Are you going to tell anyone about our intimacies this afternoon, Claire?"

"Not if you allow me to take confession in the future with your assistant, Father Sheridan."

"Thank you. I'll arrange that. Good day, Claire."

Saturday, April 25

Today, after our evening meal, I excused myself from the table and went immediately to my room. I had a strong urge to communicate with Virginia, so I sat down at my computer and composed the following note—

Dear Ginny—

I won the dare! Yesterday I went to his office dressed seductively, and he quickly managed to massage my bare ass and breasts. He also French kissed me twice. I must say that I was shocked, but you were right about him. He would have screwed me over his desk in a heartbeat. However, I stopped him in his tracks and made him promise to assign Father Sheridan to the role of my new confessor. I also told him I no longer valued his advice and would stop doing the penances he'd given me. This morning at Mass, he behaved as though nothing had happened between us in his office. How can such a learned man be so corrupt?

Hope all is well with you and that you're studying The Interior Castle.

Claire.

Within ten minutes, I received her reply.

Claire—

You've got to learn to trust my instincts--I'm actually a bit of a psychic, y'know. You were smart to switch to Father Sheridan for confession. I haven't read a word from The Interior Castle yet, just too busy with my social life. It seems like I'm falling in love with Elizabeth Metz, a young German woman who moved to our town from Berlin recently and has joined our church. How are you doing?

All my love,

Virginia

My reply to her followed quickly—

Ginny—

I've been working with some of the teachings of St. Teresa but must communicate with Sister Julianna to get clarification on several essential points. I'm surprised that you're falling in love with a German woman so soon after completing the Retreat.

Claire

Sunday, April 26

Right after Mass this morning, I spoke with Father Sheridan, requesting a time to meet. He agreed to take my confessions tomorrow after the morning service. As soon as I got home, I went directly to my computer to write Sister Julianna.

Dear Sister—

I miss your classes terribly but continue to study the works of St. Teresa. I have three questions for you--and rest assured--your answers will give me the clarification I seek.

34

1. *St. Teresa stresses the importance of soul companions. How can I find such people in my life?*

2. *She keeps stressing the need for total surrender to the will of God. How do I do that?*

3. *What is grace, and how will I know when it occurs in my life?*

I can hardly wait until my three-month trial begins.

Yours faithfully, in the arms of the Lord,

Claire.

Later that day, after supper, I received her reply.

Dear Claire,

Thank you for your email. I look forward to working with you during the upcoming three-month trial. Below are some thoughts about your questions.

> 1. *The best soul companions you could ever have are the sisters at our convent. Part of the magic of cloistered life is the association you get with others who are on a spiritual path and who love you--no matter what.*

2. To rise above the level of the ego and into the fourth mansion, you must have the courage and stamina to pledge that you will follow God's commands **no matter where they lead**. Anyone who questions their ability to do that should not even enter the castle.

3. It's essential to do the preparatory work to finally come into the presence of God, experientially. That means commitment, prayer without ceasing, fasting and loving Jesus with your whole heart. But nothing you can do will produce grace in your life. It's up to God when you'll begin to live by grace and **not by will**. Sooner or later, in your case, it **will** happen-- but Claire—you must be patient.

I hope these ideas will be of some help to you.

God bless you, Claire.

Sister J.

I immediately replied.

Dear Holy Sister—

Thank you for your prompt reply. I now have a great deal to contemplate and will keep you apprised of my progress.

Claire.

Monday, April 27

I was nervous about going into confession with Father Sheridan—but I went anyway. Once Mass was over, I stayed kneeling in prayer for fifteen minutes before entering the confessional.

Father Sheridan was waiting for me.

"Do you have sins to confess today, my child?"

"Yes, Father, I do."

"And what are they?"

"I continue to have sexual urges and cannot get rid of them."

"Have you fulfilled any of those urges?"

"I was touched intimately in two places by a man who attends our church, but against my will."

"Have you given in to your own impulses?"

"No, Father."

"That's very good, very good. It is natural to have sexual urges. The sin occurs only when you indulge them, act upon them. However, there *is* one way to neutralize them."

"How, Father?"

"When they occur, surround them in your heart with love and compassion. Let the urges be, but allow God to turn them into loving urges. Let God engulf them."

"I will work with that, Father. Thank you."

"Now, do you want to tell me who accosted you so I can follow-up on it?"

"No, Father."

"All right, are there any other confessions today?"

"No," I whispered and then slowly got up, walking back into the church for more prayer—on my knees."

Thursday, April 30

I continued craving orgasms every night but was working with Father Sheridan's solutions. It felt like love was the key, not fighting my natural urges. But one idea was haunting me. Could I have sex with Father Jessop and make it a loving act?

Yesterday, I left a note in his office mail slot requesting a meeting. I was surprised to receive an email from him today advising me to come to his quarters at 3 pm.

When I got there and entered his spacious office, he was, as usual, sitting at his expansive desk.

"How can I help you today, Claire?"

"I want to know how sex can be justified if one's motives are pure."

"Well, your question surprises me. But theoretically, if you love Jesus and turn the sex act into a prayer, it becomes purified and legitimate."

"Could you show me how that's done?"

"Right now?"

"Yes."

The priest then blushed a crimson colour, and his eyes widened considerably as he began to shake all over. I could see goosebumps on his bare arms, and he was breathing very heavily.

He got up slowly, locked his office door, and moved directly behind me.

"Do you have underwear on, Claire?"

"No."

"Please bend over my desk then, dear," he muttered. He immediately moved right up close, put his arms around my waist and lifted up my skirt. Soon a huge penis entered my vagina and began thrusting into me very hard. Fortunately, I was physically aroused and lubricated, so he was able to penetrate his cock fully, right up to his balls."

"Take it hard," he winced, slapping my right ass-cheek.

I tried to feel love for this man, but he was disgusting. He knew what he was doing was wrong, and he was treating me like a piece of meat. On the other hand, the pleasure I was experiencing was intense. I had a massive orgasm on his rod and screamed in passionate delight just before he came too and pumped large amounts of hot, white sperm deep into my body. As my vagina cooled down, I turned around, looked directly into his eyes and asked him if he was able to love God fully while he was having sex with me.

"Yes, and it was wonderful, my dear," he replied, "You can come back anytime to repeat this sacred act with me."

I then went straight home, had a shower and knelt beside my bed.

"Holy Father, please forgive me. I don't love that man--and don't believe his mind stayed on You as he was pumping me. Dear God--that act was sinful. I know it was. Please help me in my resolution to *never again have sex with someone I do not love.*"

<u>Friday, May 1</u>

I woke up with a start this morning because a loud fire truck had just raced down our street, sirens blaring. The noise had interrupted a vivid dream I was having about Virginia. She was in my bed completely naked, trying to have sex with me--but I was pushing her away forcefully.

As soon as I showered, brushed my teeth and got dressed, I sat down at my laptop to write her a note.

Dear Ginny—

I had a colourful dream about you last night, so you're on my mind this fine morning. I'm wondering how it's working out with your new German girlfriend. And, are you going deeper into The Interior Castle?

Claire

She responded, later, in the early afternoon.

Dear Claire—

Heidi and I had an argument three days ago and aren't speaking to each other right now. I've promised myself that I'll read St. Teresa's book but, for some reason, don't seem to have the time these days. You sound lonely. Why don't you drive down to Lawrenceville this weekend and stay with me at my place? I've got a small, two-bedroom apartment on the edge of Yellow Hornet River.

All my Love,

Virginia.

My response followed after supper.

Ginny—

*Let me think about it. I **am** lonely and need to talk to you about some of my friends and things that have happened lately. Father Sheridan is a great minister, and he's really helping me out.*

Claire

Saturday, May 2

I knew Father Sheridan was receiving confessions this afternoon, so I decided to see him again. I showed up at church one hour early today and sat in prayer until the line-up outside his booth had disappeared.

"Good morning, Father," I whispered through the black grate and velvet curtain between us.

"Good morning, how can I help you today?"

"I have some issues, sir."

"Would you like to confess your sins?"

"Yes."

There was a long pause before I continued. The silence was heavy.

"I've had sex again, holy Father."

"Do you love the other person involved?"

"No."

"How did you experience this event?"

"I enjoyed the physical pleasure but hated myself afterwards. It was wrong. I dislike him, and he's much older than me."

"Claire, I'm sponsoring a workshop on addictions that starts next week, and I recommend that you participate."

"Who's teaching that workshop, Father?"

"Father Pettigrew is facilitating it. He has an MA in addictions counselling and comes very highly recommended."

"Is he a Catholic priest?"

"Yes, and a good one at that, with a great reputation. He's the assistant rector at St. Peter's—the small congregation in the south side of town."

"I'll register for it, then, Father—based on your recommendation."

"That's wonderful—classes start next Friday night from 7—9:30 pm for six weeks."

"A perfect fit for me. Thank you so much, Father."

"My pleasure Claire—and please let me know how the classes go."

"Yes, I will, sir."

"May God bless and protect you always, Claire."

<u>Sunday, May 3</u>

My Mother's car was not available over the first weekend in May. Still, I had a long weekend, so decided to take the train to Lawrenceville and stay with Ginny. She was waiting for me at the station and threw her arms around me, squeezing tightly when we met.

"You look beautiful, she called out. "I love that sexy skirt you're wearing—did you stitch all those tulips on it yourself?"

"No, my mother gave it to me at Christmas, and she made it herself, by hand."

After supper and drinks at Jimmy's Diner, she drove me to her apartment. It was a clean, sparsely furnished two-bedroom unit with a great view of the river from a living room sliding glass door. There were dozens of colourful paintings hanging on just about every available space in her enclave. A large picture of Jesus with His sacred heart showing was the largest painting she had, and it dominated a whole wall.

"I didn't know you were an artist, Ginny! I love that work depicting Jesus—it's magnificent."

"Yes, that's a copy of a Rembrandt."

"Many of them are graphic."

"Well, let's just say *my* works are very realistic—but I didn't do them all. I mainly did the nudes. Do you like my *Study of Vaginas* series?"

"Well, it leaves nothing to the imagination, that's for sure. Did you copy them from photos?"

"No, I painted them from friends who were willing to pose for me."

"Can I get you a drink?" she asked.

"I'll have a diet coke--if you have one."

"Yes, of course,"

As the sunset on a distant horizon, Virginia and I got into a prolonged and personal conversation. She was drinking whiskey sours slowly, mindfully.

"I'm having second thoughts about attending the Carmelite Trial, Claire."

"Why?"

"My commitment to the spiritual path is low right now. My parents have noticed it and are nagging me a lot."

"I thought you were inspired by Sister Julianna?"

"Yes, I was. But I've also fallen in love with three people and one of them is you. Do you love me, Claire?"

"Why yes, I do, Ginny—but not in a romantic way."

"Could we sleep together again tonight? I crave being physically close to you," she asked quietly. "We don't have to do anything sexual if you don't want."

As it turned out, we kept talking for hours until it got dark outside, and we had to light candles to see where we were going. By the time we headed for bed, Virginia was definitely inebriated. She persuaded me to sleep naked with her and gave me a great deal of pleasure that night, including two volcanic orgasms. My body was massaged and kissed so deeply I thought I was going to pass out.

In the morning, I did **not** feel guilty or sinful—but something was very wrong. Yes, I did love Virginia as a sister and fellow spiritual seeker—but did **not** want to be her lover.

"I think you should reconsider and do the Trial, Ginny. It's only three months, and we can study together and really purify ourselves."

"Let me pray about it, Claire, and I'll let you know."

As soon as I got home, I knew she wasn't going to become a nun, and I also knew our friendship wouldn't last. I was still very serious about becoming a nun.

Friday, May 8

Tonight I went to the first session of my *Addictions Workshop.* As soon as I walked into the classroom, I knew it would be a valuable experience. I arrived early, and the only other person in the room was Father Pettigrew. He was a middle-aged, distinguished-looking man. He had a large smile on his face and appeared very friendly. Sitting on a metal folding chair in a circle with ten other empty chairs around him, he began to speak.

"Hello, welcome to the workshop. My name is Father Pettigrew. What's yours?" He asked me.

"Claire," I answered slowly.

"Well, there are ten participants registered, and I'm sure the others will be here soon."

By seven o'clock, nine members had shown up—five men and four women. An elderly lady came along fifteen minutes late. For the first twenty minutes, we did relaxation movements, self-massage techniques and deep breathing exercises. We ended the introduction by praying for healing.

"All addictions are sicknesses of the soul. Trying to cure an addiction without God's assistance is like trying to bake bread without an oven—it's never going to rise. Your soul is God's presence within you. When you have an addiction, part of your soul is veiled, hiding behind a black curtain, so to speak. It may feel like there's a break in your connection with God. Our essential task in this workshop is to open that curtain and get you reconnected.

This is how the padre began the seminar.

"The first thing we're going to do is share our own experiences with addiction. We'll go around the circle, so everyone gets a chance to speak. Claire, why don't you begin?"

"Alright," I said.

"It's my hope to become a Carmelite nun because I love God and never want to feel cut off from Him. But I've got a terrible sex addiction. Ever since I was fourteen years old, I've craved orgasms. My uncle raped me two days after my fourteenth birthday. It was traumatic as he was very rough with me, a virgin. But he gave me an orgasm that first time and I loved it."

"Are you becoming a nun to cure yourself of this affliction?" asked Father Pettigrew.

"That's one important reason, but there are others," I replied.

"Well, you're in the right place. I believe this workshop can help you, at this time."

"I certainly hope so," I muttered under my breath.

When everyone in the class had shared their personal experiences, the facilitator announced that we would break into pairs for an exercise.

"Your task is to get to know your partner and work on answers to a specific question. The question is, "How can God help me cure my addictions?" Now please pick a partner and arrange your chairs so that you're facing each other.

A tall youthful-looking black man immediately walked up to my chair and asked,

"Can I work with you for this session?"

"Sure," I said.

"Good because I have a sex addiction too, so I understand your particular struggle."

This man was extremely good-looking--tall, slender and muscular. He was dressed immaculately in a black sports jacket, which hung over his spotlessly clean white T-shirt.

"Do you crave orgasms, too? I asked him.

"Yes."

"How do you satisfy your sexual urges?"

"Mostly through the art of contemplation, but also with any willing woman I can find, who's also religious."

"Do you want to cure this addiction?" I asked him.

"Yes, I most definitely do."

"Well, how do you think God can help us?"

"I think we have to admit to ourselves that we don't have control over our temptations--we simply don't have the power to resist them. We need God's assistance. That would include praying, asking Him for help, committing to overcoming our urges and surrendering to His will."

"Yes, that's it! St. Teresa says that we can leave our small selves behind and enter into an actual union with God--if we're truly committed."

"Who's St. Teresa?"

"St. Teresa of Avila is a Carmelite Nun who lived in medieval times and wrote some incredible books. The one I'm currently reading is *The Interior Castle*. I find comfort in her words, and that's another reason I want to become a Carmelite Nun?"

"Tell me more, this sounds so interesting. I wanted to become a priest in my younger years but finally drifted into law. Now I work in legal-aid helping Catholics who're in trouble. But I still consider myself very religious."

"Maybe we could have supper together sometime?"

"Yes, I'd love that," he said. "How about Abby's tomorrow night at 7 pm?"

"Great—I'll meet you there, at that time.

Saturday, May 9

Abby's is a quaint family restaurant on the edge of town. Tonight it was strangely quiet—only two people were sitting there other than me.

I got there early and had just begun to check out the menu when Al arrived.

"Hi, Claire, I hope I'm not late!"

"No, I arrived early. The food here is delicious, by the way, no matter what you order."

After we gave the waitress our instructions—Al wanting the roast beef special and me just a Caesar salad—the conversation flowed.

"I looked up St. Teresa online. She was an amazing mystic, no doubt about it."

"Yes, and if you read further, you'll find out she warns us to be constantly watching for demons and temptresses sent by the devil to seduce us. But in authentic humility, we can stay vigilant. We must never assume we can always resist temptation."

"I think those demons seem to be the most powerful when it comes to our addictions, wouldn't you say?"

"How do you mean?"

"Well, I'm constantly bombarded with sex in books, movies, magazines and video clips. They get to me in my weakest moments—when I'm upset or uncomfortable."

"I can understand that. Do you want to order some wine?"

"Yeah, that'd be great."

We continued talking non-stop throughout the meal and during the dessert of blackberry pie with vanilla ice cream.

"Tell me why you want to become a nun," he asked me as the waitress handed him the bill.

"I love God and His church and believe in His word, as found in the Bible. And I know that becoming devoted to a religious life will clean up all my flaws and *purify* me."

"Yes, I'm sure it would," he replied. "Can I drive you home?"

"Sure," I replied with a sense of longing in my eyes.

I loved his BMW convertible, and he drove it with the roof down all the way home. Strong breezes rustled my hair and cooled me off. As soon as he stopped outside my home, he leaned over and kissed me fully on the lips. I then kissed him back. It was an absolutely heavenly experience—I really liked this guy!

Friday, May 15

As the workshop continued, we started dating seriously. Alvin was everything I ever imagined a man could be. He was religious, kind, generous and really handsome. His social skills were impeccable, he had tons of friends, and his intelligence was superior.

When he took me in his arms, I melted into a state of ecstasy, and it wasn't lusting. I was charmed and passionately attracted—he made me feel good about myself. And he felt the same way about me. After being together for three weeks, I knew we would become lovers, which was not a problem because I'd fallen in love with this man.

<u>Friday, May 22</u>

The first time it happened was after we played tennis for the first time on a hot summer's day.

"You're a pretty good player, Claire. But now it's time to relax. Do you want to come back to my place for drinks?" he asked me.

"Yes," I replied without hesitation.

He owned a bungalow on a quiet, dead-end street with two large maple trees in the front yard and an overflowing vegetable garden in the back. Tomatoes were his specialty, and they grew everywhere there was extra space—against the shed, by the fence and in the greenhouse.

He poured himself a Coors light and handed me a whiskey sour, and we sat on his soft crimson sofa sipping our drinks and letting a large electric fan cools us down. All of a sudden, he put his beer down and moved close to me. I was ready for his embrace, and soon we were kissing passionately. His tongue went right down my throat and I licked it. Then he put his hand up my T-shirt and started massaging my bare breasts.

"Your breasts are soft and huge," he panted, "and your nipples are long, hard, thick and erect. They're really turning me on," he spluttered.

"I'm glad you're enjoying them."

In the meantime, I slowly moved my right hand onto his hardening penis.

"Can I unzip you?"

"Let me do it," he said, as he stood up and took his jeans off and then snapped his boxers down quickly.

"I've never seen a cock this big," I gulped. "I'll never be able to get it into my mouth."

"Why don't you try?" he teased.

At that point, I stuck his penis into my mouth and sucked it gently. I was only able to get halfway down--but it felt so good. His pre-cum was filling my mouth, and it tasted fantastic, so I just kept swallowing it. Periodically, I came out and licked his hairy balls, which were the size of Mexican avocados.

"I can't take it anymore, Claire. Please sit on me."

At that point, I stood up, turned around and moved down over his prick until he was four inches deep.

"Keep going, I want the whole thing, Al," I panted.

Soon his full, thick twelve inches were in me, moving up and down as he kept massaging my tits. He moved very slowly until I begged him to speed up. He balled me like that for twenty minutes straight until I had a massive orgasm all over his tool.

"Why don't you get off me and taste your cum?" he asked.

After I licked him dry, I craved more, so I turned to face him directly and put him back inside me. Now we could look each other straight in the eyes as we fucked—which we did for another fifteen minutes."

"I'm coming again," I said.

"So am I, Claire and *I love you*."

"I love you too, Al," I screamed as I exploded again.

Just then, he squirted about a litre of sperm right up my vagina, and I could feel the hot juice moving all the way up to my uterus. It was hot, thick and sticky. He kept shooting white liquid into me for a couple of minutes.

When he was done, he kissed me deeply and hugged me while still rock hard inside. There was so much sperm in me that it began to pour out onto the colourful Persian rug below us, forming a pool.

"I've never felt that good before Al," I moaned.

"Me neither," he responded.

<u>Saturday, July 14</u>

The workshop was beneficial, but once it ended, Al and I found our own solution to lust—being in love! Love erased our raw physicality and transformed it into something beautiful, even sacred--because of the belief we both held that the sex was justified. Premarital sex was indeed banned by the church, but it didn't matter—we were too happy to feel any guilt.

Al has made love to me for twenty-two days straight, and I still can't get enough of him. We've had sex at his house, in his car, on the lawn behind our church (at night), beside a granite stone wall and under several different sets of blankets. On each occasion, I had multiple orgasms, and they were all *more* than satisfying.

Last week he asked me to move into his house, but I hesitated.

"I'm planning to become a nun, Al, and moving into your place wouldn't look good," I told him.

"Who cares what it looks like? We've got the *real* thing going," he replied.

We were together constantly when not working—at movies, churches, bookstores,

tennis courts and restaurants. We even studied *The Interior Castle* together.

I received a note from Sister Julianna two days ago and have been procrastinating my response. Her email read—

Dear Claire—

I haven't heard from you in a couple of weeks and wondered how your studies have been going and your monastic life preparation.

We miss you and look forward to your trial period.

In Christ,

Sister Julianna

Monday, July 16

I finally composed and sent my reply late last night.

Dear Sister—

I'm sorry for not writing you sooner, but I've been really busy lately. I've got a new friend, Alvin Lincoln, and we've been studying The Interior Castle *together lately.*

Here are my latest questions—

1. *St. Teresa talks a lot about the importance of soul stamina. How can I build up my stamina?*

2. *Can a sexual sin be transformed if done in love and spiritual awareness?*

I look forward to hearing from you and seeing you in September.

Claire.

"I can't wait for her answers, Al," I said to him, "and I'm sure you'll be interested in reading them too."

"Yes, I will," he whispered as he rolled close to my naked body under the covers of his bed.

Apart from two slightly irritating factors, Al was perfect. One was his tendency to flirt with beautiful women (who always seemed to be approaching him). When an attractive lady came up to him, he loved to lead them on a bit. The other was his insensitivity towards his three-year-old daughter and ex-wife.

"You don't spend much time with Julie, Al," I commented.

"No—her mother's now got a boyfriend, and I don't want to confuse her with two fathers," he answered. "Besides, her mother's quite hostile towards me."

"Did you make any efforts to reconcile with her?"

"No, Claire—she's toxic for me."

Later, I received Sister Julianna's latest email.

Dear Claire—

I'm happy that you've found a friend who's also interested in the work of St. Teresa. Perhaps he's a soul mate. Here are my responses to your questions.

1. *Soul stamina is critically important. For extroverted and passionate people like yourself, I recommend listening to tapes on the Word of God whenever you're wavering. Let those tapes lead you into a peaceful silence. As it happens, I have a full set of cassette tapes on The Interior Castle, which I can loan you if you like.*

2. *Love transforms anything. St. Augustine said, "Love, then do whatever you want."*

Soon you'll be back in an enclosed community dedicated to experiencing the Lord's truth.

God Bless You,

Sister Julianna

Wednesday, July 18

I talked to Al about Julianna's email this morning.

"I'm inspired by the Sister's teaching that love transforms everything," I said and went on, "I feel changed by being in a relationship with you. Sex has stopped being an addiction based on lust—now it's a creative expression of my love. Premarital sex is against the teaching of the church, but I don't care—for me, love justifies it, purifies it."

"I feel the same way, Claire."

"Would you like to listen to those tapes on *The Interior Castle*?"

"Yes, very much so."

After that conversation, I was able to respond to Sister Julianna's correspondence.

Dear Holy Sister—

Thank you for yesterday's note. What you say about love corresponds precisely with what I'm experiencing in many aspects of my life right now.

My friend and I are very enthusiastic about listening to those tapes you mentioned. It's something we can do together, and both enjoy.

Thank you for that offer.

Faithfully,

Claire.

Wednesday, August 1

At first, I was shocked and angry when my pregnancy test came back positive. However, once I calmed down, the situation's positives revealed themselves to me.

Why panic? This was life telling me I would become a happy wife and Mother—not a nun. I could still be devoutly religious and raise a child of God—straight in the ways of the Lord.

So I called Al and left a message on his cell phone.

"You'll be happy to hear that you're going to become a father for the second time. And yes—I've decided to take you up on your offer and move in with you as soon as possible. I'm 99% certain that the baby's yours. (Do you remember me telling you that a member of my church--that I don't like--accosted me? Well, that only happened once.)

Friday, August 3

Strangely, I didn't hear back from Al for almost two days. Finally, today, he sent me an email. It read—

Dearest Claire—

Sorry I didn't get back to you right away, but I've been very, very busy with family matters for the past two days.

It looks like my ex-wife, and I are getting back together. She's broken up with her boyfriend and wants our daughter to have her real father around her. That'll give me an opportunity to spend quality time with Julie--on a regular basis.

Congratulations on the pregnancy! You'll be a great mother. As time passes, let me know what I can do to support you. But for now, it's best we don't see each other until everything settles down.

Affectionately,

Al

Wednesday, August 15

It took me over a week to secure an interview for my abortion. Unfortunately, I was going to have to drive all the way to Sioux City to get it done. Thanks to certain religious zealots, we no longer have a Family Planning Clinic in our town. Dr. Jerry Waldran was shot dead while walking to work last year and, after that, our clinic was closed permanently. Luckily, I *was* approved for a fetus removal, and the procedure was scheduled for August 30 at the Sioux City Family Planning Clinic.

Ever since hearing from Alvin, I've been pouring over key passages in *The Interior Castle*. Some are so important I memorized them.

This morning I sent Sister Julianna an email.

Dear Sister—

Due to recent events, I've reached an inflection point. My commitment to becoming a Carmelite has been finalized. I yearn for the days of peace, asceticism, celibacy and prayer that await me at the monastery. I can't wait to see you, and all the sisters, in just three short weeks. In the meantime, I shall 'let nothing disturb me' as I pray without ceasing.

In Christ,

Claire

Cleo

On the way back from the *Mexicali*, Cleo stopped at a liquor store with her nephew to pick up a bottle of Chardonnay and some mango incense sticks. Once they arrived back at her apartment, she lit several sand-candles and three sticks of the incense before carefully opening the wine and pouring it into two tall, thin glasses.

Josh and Cleo talked about growing up in the fifties and playing sports with all the cousins. She told him he was always a happy child, and she always loved it when he came over to play with her sons. They laughed and joked, enjoying the setting sun and cool breeze that flowed across Cleo's deck into the living room.

When the two wine glasses were empty, Cleo got up and went into her bedroom, soon emerging in a long velvet robe, and whispered, "I'm going to have a shower. Pour yourself another glass of wine while I get cleaned up."

Josh got up slowly and ambled towards the picture window that looked out over the sea as the tide came in. By this time, the lighting was dim, so he turned on a lamp and sat back on her long over-stuffed, mellow-red sofa. A Leonard Cohen cassette tape was playing softly in the background. He heard Cleo shuffling down the hall behind him and turned to speak to her just as his favourite tune, *Suzanne*, started playing.

She entered the living room and moved to the couch's left side, slowly placing her rear end on its wide arm. She was young-looking for someone fifty-five, and Josh felt slightly aroused.

"This is strange," he thought.

Suddenly he noticed that her robe was hanging open. The top half of her large, alabaster-white breasts were clearly visible. Josh stared at her, riveted to her pose, transfixed by her raw sexuality. She slid down onto the seat beside him.

"Josh, are you staring at my breasts?"

"Well, sort of."

Pausing and smiling, she asked him, "Would you like to touch them?"

He was frozen and felt paralyzed. He couldn't speak, nor could he turn his eyes away from his aunt's body. She smelled strongly of the sweet aroma of Emeraude.

"It's okay, you need to relax and touching me will take your mind off Susan," she said clearly. "It must be hard on you to be without a woman right now. But if you do touch them, please be gentle---they're very sensitive."

Josh slowly reached over and tenderly stroked her right breast, pulling her gown down, so they were both fully exposed. Cleo was very well endowed. Slowly her thick, dark-brown nipples hardened and stood erect--over an inch high on each massive mammary. As he massaged her, she moaned, leaned back and loosed the cord around her waist. After that, Josh was able to rub both tits and occasionally hold them firmly while he stared at them and admired just how beautiful they were.

"That feels so nice, Honey. Keep rubbing me like that, only a bit slower," she said as she opened the knot in the cord around her robe. It fell open at the bottom, revealing her thighs, legs, hairy triangle and bare feet. Josh then moved his right hand down to her right thigh and slowly massaged it with real sensitivity.

"Oh boy, you're really turning me on now, Josh—don't stop."

Soon his index finger was on her vagina, moving inside it-- ever so slightly. He parted her black-grey mound of pubic hair to please her and then spread her legs so that they were wide open. Cleo moaned deeply and leaned back on the sofa.

"Josh, can you take your bathing suit off so I can touch *you*?" she muttered as he continued the massage of her cunt.

He then stood up in front of her, gingerly pulled his shorts down to his ankles, and stepped right out of them.

She stared right at him without blinking.

"Honey, you're massive---thick *and* long. I've never seen anything so big, and trust me, I've seen hundreds of cocks."

"Thank you," said Josh. "You can touch it if you want."

Cleo put her right hand on Josh's penis and gripped it firmly. Then she started massaging his testicles with a slow circular motion.

"Can I put it into your mouth, Cleo?"

"Perhaps later, but for now, just *relax*," she said.

Josh stepped in very close to her as she began to caress his engorged member deftly. Pre-cum began to drip onto the floor, and he groaned in ecstasy. His cock was soaking wet, and he ached to place it into her open, waiting mouth. Sperm splashed all over her, spilling down onto her enormous breasts and nipples.

"See if you can take the whole thing in your mouth, please, Cleo," he begged as he moved closer—within an inch of her red-lipsticked lips.

"Josh, my Gawd, it's at least eleven inches long and three inches wide. It'll never fit---but I'll try if that's what it's going to take to make you happy."

She then grabbed the cheeks of his ass with both hands and pulled him forward. Josh began thrusting his prick back and forth inside her lips as they tightly grasped his full width. Then he moved slower and tried to put his entire length inside of her. Slowly, he was making progress. At one point, she took him all the way down until his balls brushed her lips.

"Now use your tongue," he yelped.

Sperm continued to pour out of her mouth, covering her lower face and dripping down onto her boobs and legs. She was now soaking wet.

"Cleo, I'm going to explode," he exclaimed.

"Okay, darling, come right into my mouth," she said. "I'd love to swallow your whole load." Rubbing her jaw, she slid his cock back into her mouth.

Suddenly, Josh's body jerked and pulsated, and he ejaculated his full load directly into her mouth. High-pressured streams of hot sperm smashed against the back of her throat and flowed right down the passageways into her stomach. She held him tightly with her lips locked onto him until he was wholly finished with his orgasm. He came and came and came. His balls produced over a litre of liquid, and she swallowed every last drop.

"Oh wow," he moaned and finally pulled himself out of her.

"Your juice tasted delicious," she exclaimed, "You obviously haven't had sex for a long, long time."

"It's been over a year," he shared.

They talked for a few minutes before Josh had an urge to kiss his aunt, so he leaned over and put his mouth right on hers. Then he threw caution to the wind and stuck his tongue right down her throat. She was so excited by this action that she reciprocated and put her tongue into him. There they were—

both completely naked and necking passionately. They continued kissing for over half an hour before Josh pulled away and moaned,

"You make me so horny, Cleo--it was never like this with Sue. She didn't really like sex that much, but you love it! Thank you for servicing me so completely."

"You're welcome, sweetheart," she responded, "But there's still something missing for me."

"What's that?"

"I'd like you to put that monster cock into my cunt, *right now*? Can you get it hard again?"

Josh answered, "Let me try." Immediately his prick was hard as a rock standing fully erect again--straight and thick. He sat down on the couch and pulled her around so she stood directly in front of him.

"Sit on me," he ordered.

She moved close and lifted both her legs onto the couch, wrapping them around his sweaty body. Then she slowly lowered herself right onto his massive member, facing him directly—staring into his wide-open eyes. His penis slid easily into her as she was really wet and turned on. He was able to penetrate her right up to the hilt, and she loved it.

"Do it harder," she pleaded. "It feels so good. Keep screwing me and kiss me. Don't stop. Fuck me like a bull."

"Oh no, I'm coming again," he screamed. "Okay, dear, blow your load again. I want all of it. And I'm coming too!"

Suddenly Josh exploded for the second time--filling her vagina with hot, white sperm. She could feel its warmth enter her and move all the way up to her stomach. The excess slowly began to dribble out just as her juices flowed all over his manhood.

"Stay in me," she moaned, "Don't pull out. I love you in me."

Josh kept his dick inside of Cleo for over an hour. They kept whispering to each other and necking. Often their eyes met, and glances held. Feelings of love and devotion welled up inside them both.

"You can fuck me any time you want, night or day," Cleo said after a long pause.

"Just come to my apartment, knock on the door and state your name. I'll let you in, and you can do whatever you want to me."

"I'll do that, Cleo, and by the way, I *do* love you. How often do you like having sex—I would never want to overdo it."

"How 'bout every day?"

Mother Knows Best

In June 1963, James R. Wilson and his wife Roxanne bought a character home that was apparently haunted—and they couldn't care less about any of the scary rumours. He was a hard-bitten lawyer who didn't believe in ghosts, and she was an ex-hippy who fully embraced the idea that spirits could be friendly if treated well.

Their daughter, Corinne, was one of my sister's best friends growing up. We lived in the same neighbourhood in Veriton as the Wilson's. It was an area of town that used to be inhabited by upper-class gentry. Still, many of their over-sized Tudor dwellings had become derelict and seedy over time. The Wilson estate sat on an acre of land at the end of a quiet cul-de-sac. Towering Gary Oak trees stood near thick bushes of ivy and a crumbling stone wall that used to circumvent the entire property. Our place was more modest—a rectangular bungalow five blocks to the west on a quiet road near Stadium Park. It had three bedrooms, one bathroom, a living room and an ample crawl space six feet high with lots of spiders.

Behind the Wilson land on Berkshire Street stood a High-Anglican church with a steeple almost fifty feet high. To the east, beside it were three massive grass hockey fields owned by St. Catherine's Academy for Girls—an institution both Corrine and my sister Faith attended from kindergarten right through Grade 12.

Although Faith and I were never very close, it was a real bonus that she had many school friends two years younger than me. As we got older and matured sexually, there were many opportunities to engage physically with some of them. Sometimes I got busted for necking a hot pal of my sister's or hugging another too closely at a birthday party. But my most outlandish sins involved Corinne.

By the time she was eighteen, she'd become a woman in every sense of the word. She was smart as a whip--having been a straight-A student her whole life—but shallow emotionally. You could even call her cold and calculating. Her parents were wealthy and had spoiled her hopelessly. For example, she had over one hundred dresses in her bedroom closet—most of which she never wore. She was five feet ten inches tall and weighed ninety-one pounds, soaking wet. Although her chest was flat, she had a definite sexual presence and could be openly flirtatious. Her ass was small, taut and swayed slightly when she walked. As it turned out, under that cool, sharp, snobby exterior, a raging nymphomaniac lay hidden.

I first found out about her sexual appetites when I was twenty-one years old, and she was nineteen. One evening my sister and I were having drinks and discussing our father's estate. Over the course of the evening, Faith had become outrageously drunk.

"Are you still close to Corinne?" I asked her, feeling a bit tipsy myself.

"No, I donna see har mush anymore. Not after I found out, she's a fuckin' slut.'

"How do you mean?"

"She'll fuck anything that walks but has na feelins for anyone. I saw ha screw two guys at the same pahty—one after t'other—and they both had galfriends there."

A few weeks later, I happened to bump into Corinne at Murdoch's Book Store on Orchard Street—a small, locally-owned shop where she worked as a bookseller.

"Oh, hi Corinne," I said casually to her as she sat behind the counter.

"Hello John, how are you?"

"Just fine, and you?"

"Well, I just broke up with my latest boyfriend, but otherwise, things are good."

"How's your Mom doing?"

"Having trouble coping since Dad died. She can't accept the fact that a forty-eight-year-old man could suddenly have a heart attack and fall down dead. The only thing keeping her sane is her fortune-telling and the reading of her tarot cards."

"Fortune-telling?"

"Yeah, she's become a professional fortune-teller and travels to psychic healing fairs all over the county. I've no idea why because Mom doesn't need the money. Dad had a generous life insurance policy, and their home was paid for years ago."

"Are you living with her?"

"Yeah, for now. I moved back in when Butch and I split--but hopefully, it won't be for long—she drives me crazy. Why don't you drop by one evening to cheer her up? She always speaks well of you."

"Now that sounds like a great idea."

Fifteen days later, I walked up the long flight of granite stairs leading to the Wilson's front door and banged the black cast-iron knocker hard three times. It was a warm summer's night, and an orange sun was setting—sending a golden hue all around the old mansion.

"Hi John," greeted Corinne as the front door creaked open, "Good to see you. C'mon in—Mom's gone to the liquor store but should be back any minute. I'm just listening to music in my bedroom, d'ya want to join me?"

"Sure, sounds good. I just came by to give your Mom these chocolates," I replied—holding up a big box of Rowntree Soft Caramels.

I then followed Corinne through the high-vaulted, mahogany-panelled lobby and along a narrow passageway that led to a steep-circling set of stairs. At the top of those stairs, across from an inlaid oak floor, was the door to her bedroom. The room was small and over-furnished, so the space was decidedly cramped once we both were inside. She sat down on her puffy eiderdown, pulled the earphones out of her CD player and turned on some *Peter, Paul and Mary* music.

The whole scene was very relaxing until I noticed her skirt had slipped up to the top of her thighs, and she had no panties on. Her curly, black-haired pubic area was clearly visible while she sat there rocking back and forth with her eyes closed.

Without hesitating, I started massaging her soaking wet mound with my right hand. She moaned slightly but didn't open her eyes and did nothing to stop me or slow me down. Corrine was so inviting I couldn't resist going down on her. Before long, my tongue was fully two inches inside her body, biting and licking her clit.

Two minutes later, she screamed, "Shit, I'm coming," and then copious amounts of love-juice squirted all over my face.

"That was nice, John, thank-you. But I want you to fuck me now," she stated matter-of-factly.

I wasted no time ripping my pants off and stroking my seven-inch penis until it was fully erect.

"Lie down on my bed," she ordered, "I wanna climb on top of you."

I wasn't the best lover in the world but did have good staying power. My cock was only slightly larger than average, but I was a hockey player in great shape. I had the ability to screw a horny chick for up to an hour before ejaculating.

Corrine put my member into her hot, wet vagina and rode it hard for thirty-eight minutes. (I timed it.) She took me right down to the balls and had three powerful orgasms during the time we screwed. I was enjoying myself too because my hands were gripping her tiny ass hard as she humped up and down—and she was extremely tight, which sent my dick into an ecstatic state. Finally, I exploded into her lower body, pumping a quart of sperm that went all the way up to her cervix.

I happened to glance toward the open bedroom door-- just as my cock left Corinne's opening--and was utterly shocked to see Mrs. Wilson standing in the doorway. She had been watching her daughter ravage me in a very aggressive way. As soon as she saw me looking at her, and before Corinne could notice anything out of place, she instantly disappeared.

"That was nice, John. You can last longer than anyone I've ever fucked. We should do this again sometime."

"That'd be nice," I replied.

I couldn't get Corinne out of my mind for the following week. Not that there was any love lost between us or even affection—but the physical act of having her ball me to a wild climax was extremely exciting. She was a sex machine—tight, always horny—ready to fuck anyone at a moment's notice.

Two weeks later, I simply had to go back to the Wilson's, but Roxanne answered the door this time.

"Hi Mrs. Wilson, did you get the chocolates I brought by a fortnight ago? I gave them to Corinne to give to you."

"No, John, I didn't—Corinne's very forgetful at times--but it was nice of you to think of me."

"Is Corrine home?"

"No, she moved in with Jake Silver yesterday, which bothers me a lot."

"Why?"

"He's in a biker gang and does drugs."

"Oh, that *is* a concern."

"Well, come in, John, I'd like to read your fortune."

"Okay, that'd be fun. Corinne told me you'd become a fortune teller."

Roxanne Wilson then led me into her kitchen, and we sat down at a long monastery table with six oversized chairs. She was fifty years old and not unattractive. She was indeed a bit plump, but her beautiful green eyes, open, friendly face and gigantic breasts made her easy to look at. Her shoulders and arms were well-proportioned. The truth is she was a very voluptuous woman.

That day she wore a pink, cotton moo-moo covering her physical being completely--from the neck down.

Through the expansive windows, I could see lush vegetation outside—leafy oak trees, bright green ferns and out-of-control blackberry bushes growing up to forty feet tall.

"Have you ever had your fortune told before, John?"

"No, I haven't."

"You'll enjoy this then," she said, taking hold of my right hand and staring at it.

"You're going to fall in love with an older lady shortly, and she'll become the love of your life. She'll make you very happy for a long time."

"Are you sure about that?"

"Yes, your romance line is thick and full of blood."

"I didn't know you were attracted to older women, John."

"I didn't either, until now," I stuttered.

80

Before she could continue with my reading, I asked her,

"How are you making out these days as a single person?"

"John, I'll be honest with you. I'm starting to get used to living alone, but it's hard with no man around the house."

"What do you miss the most?"

"Sex, John. Clive was a powerful lover, and his sexual prowess made life interesting for me. He made love to me every single day of our marriage."

"Wow, that's a lot of love-making, Mrs. Wilson!"

"Well, I'm an over-sexed person, so it worked well for me."

"Over-sexed—what does that mean?"

"I'm addicted to orgasms--but not with just anyone. I mean, before I go to bed with someone, I have to feel love for them."

"That makes sense, Mrs. Wilson."

"John, could you start calling me Roxanne or Roxie—Mrs. Wilson sounds too formal."

"Sure, not a problem Roxie."

"John, did you know I'm actually experiencing love feelings for you *right now*? And I'd like to be *really* candid with you. Would you be alright with that?"

"Yes, of course."

"I saw you fucking my daughter for over an hour recently, and that totally impressed and excited me. Clive could only go for five or six minutes before he came. I'm feeling aroused sexually at the moment and want you to make love to me. Will you do that?--I'm so horny."

"If you want me *that* badly, I could try, Roxie. Are you *sure* you *really* want it?"

"Yes, please, please... let's do it *now*."

She then took my hand and walked me down a long hall which led to the master bedroom. That room was very spacious and had a king-sized bed with carved posts and a wide canopy hovering over it, above a magnificent Persian quilt.

"Strip naked and lie down on my bed, John; I'm going to massage your back."

As it turned out, Roxie was a masterful masseuse. After coating my back, rear-end and legs with olive oil, she began to massage every pore, crevice and tight spot on the back of my body. It felt like a wave of healing electric currents were running through me—making me so relaxed that I actually fell asleep. Sometime later, Roxie tapped my shoulder and whispered into my ear,

"Roll over onto your back now so I can work on the *front* of your physique."

By this time, I felt rested but alive with some kind of powerful psychic energy buzzing around inside me. Before long, Roxie was massaging my cock slowly, mindfully and erotically.

"You've got a lovely penis, my dear," she whispered, "And I'm going to start sucking very soon."

All of a sudden, my prick was covered by a large, warm mouth, and I could feel a wet tongue licking it as Roxie put my entire member into her mouth, right down to the balls.

Ten minutes later, I moaned,

"If you keep doing that, I'm going to shoot sperm into your mouth, Roxie."

"I'd love you to do that," she said coolly, pulling off me temporarily. But soon, she was back at work.

"Oh no," I screamed, "I'm coming," as rope after rope of hot jizz squirted out of me, assaulting the back of her throat, every drop of which slid down her throat into an awaiting stomach.

"Wow, that was fantastic," Mrs. Wilson," I mumbled. "I've never had head *that good* before."

"I'm glad you liked it, Honey. Now, are you still going to be able to make love to me?"

"Let me try."

Because my cock was still rock-hard, I was able to pull Roxie on top of me and insert myself into her wet, open vagina. Like Corinne, she was now on top of me as I started to fuck.

"You're wonderful," she shouted, "But please slow down. I want you to take me lovingly. John, *I love you*."

I was then able to make love to Roxanne Wilson for forty-two minutes straight without stopping once. She kept coming on my hard dick—perhaps five or six times—moaning as she twitched and exploded on me each time, squirting her love juices all over me. By the time I finally had my second orgasm, the sheets were soaking wet.

"I'm coming again, Roxie," I screamed and then shot another litre of sperm out the top of my cock—this time into her hot, wet cunt. Soon, streams of creamy white liquid were dripping out of her--making the bed even wetter.

"John, I've never come more than once before during love-making, in my entire life. That was heavenly. You totally satisfy me."

After I cleaned myself up and started to get dressed, I looked around Roxie's bedroom. There were exquisite potted ferns all along one wall and a full-height palm tree sitting beside the entrance to her ensuite. Under that tree sat a beautifully carved statue of the Buddha that must have been at least four feet tall. Strangely, this sacred figure had a huge red stone implanted in its forehead and two other ones like it in the palms of each one of his open hands. He sat motionless in the full lotus position.

"Roxie," I exclaimed, "That Buddha statue is exquisite."

"Yes, it is. Clive bought it for me in Hawaii—paid $55,000.00. Do you see those sparkling red stones in it?"

"Yes."

"They're rubies."

"Oh my God, that Buddha takes my breath away. He *inspires* me."

"Are you a Buddhist?"

"No, but I've read over a hundred books on the Buddhist way of life, and I try to follow many of their teachings."

"Well, I'm glad you like the carving—so do I."

"Let's go into the kitchen, John and have some wine."

"That sounds like a wonderful idea."

"Good—I have a proposal to make to you—but let's relax a bit first."

Roxie and I sat at the monastery table and began drinking very costly red wine out of beautiful, tall, hand-cut crystal glasses.

"I'd like to give you that Buddha statue. Would you like it?"

"YES—absolutely!"

"If I do, there are certain things I'd ask for in return."

"I'm all ears, Mrs. Wil...Roxie..."

"I'm very lonely now and need a man. All I want you to do is move into my home for six months. You'll pay no rent, and all your food and drink requirements will be provided free of charge—and I'm a fantastic cook. You'll have to sleep in my bed and make love to me at least *once every day*. If, after six months, you want to end the agreement—that'll be fine. But if you want to stay permanently at that point, I'd be overjoyed. I've had all of this written into a contract. Will you sign it?"

"As I've come to realize, a *mother always knows what's best*. Of course, I'll sign it."

A Virility Boost

Sam Sullivan's wife was a model of virtue and an obedient woman. Her conforming middle-class values were absolute, but she craved a diet of constant sex for one flaw.

For the most part, Sam was able to satisfy her nymphomania through fifty years of harmonious marriage. But by the time he was seventy, Nancy Sullivan's husband was losing his potency. Despite daily doses of testosterone gel and the regular use of Viagra, his sexual prowess was failing. The fact that he'd had his prostate removed didn't help matters.

Nancy never complained and never stopped behaving like a loving wife. She attended church services twice a week with Sam, regularly golfed with their best friends in a foursome and cooked gourmet meals for her husband every night of the week.

Sam was sixty-eight years old and had recently retired from his job as a painter for the City of Burnaby. He played squash three times a week, ate an enriched diet and napped during the day whenever he felt tired. The bottom line was--he was still in good physical shape.

"I'm sorry I couldn't get it up last night, Darling—you were so horny. It's just that I was exhausted from playing squash for three hours."

"Honey, that's not a problem at all—as a matter of fact, I fell asleep before you!"

"Nancy, we've never had a fight in our marriage, and I don't want my sexual challenges to change that."

"Don't worry, you're still the best husband in the world."

"Thank you, dear, but I know your sex drive hasn't waned, and you're still a gorgeous, voluptuous woman."

As a matter of fact, Nancy could still turn heads at the age of sixty-seven. She looked no older than forty-five, had enormous breasts with thick nipples, a tiny waist and long strawberry-blonde hair, with no gray. However, Nancy was a devout evangelical Christian and believed sex was only meant to occur between a man and his wife. She also believed that a good wife's role was to obey her husband in every possible way. She'd forever be the heart of their family while he was the head.

One night, a twenty-year-old university student joined Sam's squash group because Conn Smith was sick. While showering after the game, Sam noticed that this young fellow, Jack Turner, was quite virile and at the peak of his sexual powers.

"How'd you like to join me for a beer?" he asked him.

"Sure, that'd be great," replied Jack.

After a few drinks at the Red Star, Jack began to open up.

"I'm in a tough situation, Sam. My girlfriend recently threw me out of her condo, and I lost my part-time waiter's job due to Covid—19."

"Where are you living now?" asked Sam.

"I'm staying with my Mom in her RV—but she's got a new boyfriend and has asked me to leave by the end of the week—so I've been hunting for a cheap place to rent."

"While you're looking, you can stay with my wife and me. We've got a spare bedroom in the basement and, if you can help me with yard work, I won't charge you any rent! We can also provide you food for free in that temporary deal."

"Wow—that sounds fantastic, Sam. When can I move in?"

"How about tomorrow?"

"What time?"

"Come by for supper at 6 pm."

"I'll be there with bells on!"

Jack fit perfectly into the lifestyle of the Sullivan's. He spent most of his time studying when home and didn't hesitate to help Sam with the gardening and any other required household chores that came up. Nancy made an effort to prepare foods for him that he specifically loved.

Two weeks after Jack moved in, Sam knocked on his bedroom door late one night.

"Can I come in?"

"Sure, by all means."

"Y'know we're really pleased with the way everything's working out with you living here—but I'd like to ask you to do me one favour."

"Sure Sam—what is it?"

"I'd like you to have sex with my wife."

"Pardon me?" Jack shot back, fidgeting in his chair, and blushing.

"I know it sounds crazy, but Nancy has a super-sized, hyper-sensitive clitoris and craves hard intercourse every day. She's been known to have five orgasms during a single session. But Jack, I can no longer satisfy her. Due to prostate issues, I've become impotent."

"But wouldn't it make you jealous?"

"Not at all--I've made love to my wife just about every night for fifty years, and I don't want to deprive her anymore of something that gives her so much bliss."

"But she's a very religious woman, Sam—to her, adultery's a mortal sin."

"Not if I demand that she do it. Now look, it's her birthday this Friday, and I want to tell her my present this year is hard, prolonged sex with you. Can you help me out with this?"

"Well, I do find your wife attractive and, despite the fact that she wears baggy

clothes, I can see she's still got a great figure."

"You'll do it then?"

"If you absolutely insist."

"I do."

The next night, Sam snuggled up to his wife in bed and moved his right hand inside the extra-large Bonnie Henry T-Shirt she'd worn to bed. As he massaged her over-sized breasts, she began to breathe heavily and sigh with pleasure. Soon he was caressing her Mound of Venus and rubbing her clit with dexterity.

"I'm goin' come, Jack, don't stop," she moaned.

After exploding on his index finger, she reached down in search of his cock, but Jack intercepted her and said, "Not tonight, Darling. I'm still not quite ready. But I *will* have a wonderful present for your body tomorrow. After all, it'll be your birthday."

"More blue pills?"

"No, dear--I've arranged for Jack to make love to you. He's got a young penis that's over eleven inches long and three inches wide, and his testicles are the size of Sunkist oranges in August."

"I couldn't let him do that. You're my husband, and I'd never cheat on you."

"It's not cheating if I know about it and allow it. But, honey, I'm *demanding* that you let this happen. I love you and feel terrible that you've lost so much pleasure in your life due to my failings. Now—tomorrow night come to bed naked. Jack will join you at 10 pm. I'll be in the bedroom next door if anything goes wrong."

The next night, at 10 pm, Jack slipped into the master bedroom and jumped into Nancy's bed. He quickly began massaging her naked breasts and was soon sucking her hardened, thick, erect nipples. At first, Nancy just lay there like a corpse, but when Jack started stroking her pubic area, she came alive.

Sam could hear Jack groaning next door, so he got up and peeked into this wife's bedroom. At that point, Jack had his entire length stuck right down his wife's throat as she rubbed his balls, which were pressing up against her chin. A steady stream of pre-cum poured out of her mouth and dripped onto her heaving tits. He went back to bed, but his sleep was soon interrupted by loud screaming, so he had to have another look at his wife. She was lying naked on their bed as Jack fucked her—driving his monster prick deep inside her-- over and over again.

"Harder, Jack, do it harder," she begged while bouncing up and down.

Strangely, this activity aroused Sam sexually. He noticed that his penis was fully erect—something that hadn't happened for over a year.

Jack balled his wife for forty-seven minutes before shooting a quart of hot, creamy sperm into her body. During this marathon, Nancy experienced six mind-blowing orgasms.

The minute Jack went back downstairs, Sam walked straight into the master bedroom and climbed into bed.

"I'm horny, darling—feel my cock."

"Wow—you're as hard as a rock, dear. Please make love to me right *now*."

Nancy then rolled on top of her husband and inserted his adequate tool deep inside her vagina, which was still full of Jack's hot juices. Two minutes later, Sam released himself inside his wife, sending a bit of sperm deep into her crevice so that it mixed with Jack's.

"I came too, sweetheart," she whispered, "And it was wonderful. What made you so turned on?"

"When I saw Jack screwing you, I got totally aroused. Did you like your birthday presents?"

"Yes, I did."

"Then let's try this again tomorrow night."

"Are you sure that's what you *really* want, Sam?"

"Yes--will you have sex with *both* of us again?"

"Only if you *demand* it!"

"Well, I *do* demand it," said Sam, who was slowly falling asleep inside his wife's loving arms."

The Gift

One of the few things my wife Jeni and I have in common is our love of pornographic videos. Every Wednesday and Saturday night—right before sex—we watch a full-length adult movie. That sets the stage for passionate lovemaking.

Last summer, we watched James Engine, a poor actor but very well-hung black man, have rough intercourse with a woman twice his age—while her husband watched.

"Would you ever like to do something like that, Honey?" I asked Jeni.

"How do you mean?"

"Get fucked by a twelve-inch penis while I watch."

"I've never thought about that, Bill. Would you like to watch me do it?"

"Maybe, if I was in the right mood."

In early October, right after we'd watched Jodi West screw her black son-in-law and beg him not to tell her new husband, Jeni said,

"I might try that black cock—*just once*-- but only if you asked me to and watched the whole event."

"Let's put an ad in *Local Swingers* and see what happens. This could add some spark to our sex life," I replied.

That ad was placed two days later and read,

Happy married couple seeks well-endowed black man for passionate adventures. billjeni@yafew.com

To our amazement, we received twelve replies within forty-eight hours, seven of which looked promising. The one we chose to follow-up on was from Carter Smith, whose response stated,

I'm a football player who'd like to make you both happy. Just give me one chance, you won't regret it. I'm clean, friendly, humorous and very big, where it counts. Cartsmith@hawtmale.com

Carter came into our home on October 27th. He was a twenty-six-year-old former football player; six foot seven inches tall, two hundred twenty pounds.

I opened the front door, shook his large, bulbous hand and said,

"Come join us in the hot tub, Carter. It's under a canopy on the deck out back."

Jeni was sitting in the tub naked from the waist up, and our guest could clearly see her naturally over-sized breasts jiggling whenever she moved.

"Would you like a drink?" I asked.

"A cold beer would hit the spot if you have one," he replied as he sat down.

"Coming right up, my friend. I hear you're a football player,"

"Yes--played in the NFL for two years."

"What do you do for a living now?"

"I used to work as a stripper at Pluto's, but the pandemic came along and knocked me completely out of work."

"I'm sorry to hear that, but let me introduce you to my wife."

"Jeni, I'd like you to meet Carter, my new friend."

"Hi Carter, I can tell you've played some vigorous sports because your shoulders and biceps are so muscular and well-developed."

"Thank you, Ma'am."

"Not Ma'am – Jeni, please."

"Jeni."

"Now relax, take off your shirt and sit down in that chair by the heater."

Carter pulled off his sweater and threw it over the back of the chair. Jeni continued, "Wow, I've never seen skin so smooth, tight and dark –but may I ask what kind of football injury would cause all those scars on your right arm?"

"I grew up in a Chicago slum, and it got pretty rough there at times."

"Oh, dear. I'm sorry to bring that to mind for you. I was thinking surgery scars, and Bill and I both have some of those. "

"Well," I said, handing Carter another beer, "we were hoping to have some fun tonight..."

"What would you like me to do?"

"I'm not sure--Bill and I are new to this kind of thing."

"Do you mind if we just talk for a bit? I'm feeling very depressed right now."

"Why on earth would you be depressed? Queried Jeni.

"My favourite uncle died from Covid last week. He was only 54 years old."

"How did that happen?"

"He went to a local karaoke bar with some friends and picked it up. He was singing with strange people all night, and y'know what--terrible things always seem to happen to him when he drinks too much. I couldn't even tell him I loved him at the end because he was isolated in the hospital."

"Hey, Carter, don't cry," I whispered as tears plopped into the tub. "There's nothing you could have done to save him."

"Take off your track pants and sit beside me in the tub," interjected my wife. "It's hot in here, and I don't know if I can make you feel better, but I'm going to try."

When Carter was nude, he was a sight to behold. He had large glistening black eyes and close-cropped hair. His classical Caribbean face was imposing with a long, slender nose and well-defined chin. His shoulders were broad, his waist was narrow, and his penis hung all the way down to his knees. I watched him slip into the bubbly water and snuggle up close to Jeni. Her eyes were popping out of her head as she said,

"Do you mind if I massage Carter's neck and shoulders, Billy?"

"No, not at all," I said, "Our friend needs lots of support right now."

"Your hand feels wonderful, Jeni," he moaned, "But I still can't handle why this pandemic is killing so many people."

"I'm just trying to relax you and encourage you to feel welcome and wanted. What you've been through lately is very heartbreaking. Sooner than later, the virus will leave us. In the meantime, the separation from loved ones is very hard on our mental health."

"You're very wise and kind, Jeni."

"You remind me of our youngest son, Carter, so my heart goes out to you. I want to give you a loving kiss now to ease your grief and calm you down."

"That's a great idea," I added, "Make him feel loved, Honey."

Jeni then pulled Carter's neck down so that his mouth was next to hers and gave him a soft kiss directly on the lips.

"Thank you," he said with a smile. "Now I'm going to kiss you back."

Seeing my wife necking with a giant black man started to turn me on, so I moved closer to get a better view. Smells of sweat mixed with lipstick and perfume heightened the eroticism.

"I love it when you stick your tongue down my throat, Carter," moaned Jeni.

"And I love it when you put yours down mine," he added.

Jeni was kissing him passionately, pouring her nurturing love deep into the black man's body. She felt his suffering and wanted to take it away. After forty-five minutes of continuous French kissing, Jeni said,

"Let me massage your thighs now—that'll make you really loosen up."

"Your hands are making my legs go limp, and all the tension is leaving my *entire* lower body," sighed Carter as he lay his head back against the fence and closed his eyes.

"Can I rub his penis now, Billy?"

"Yes—do it—that'll make him feel like he's part of the family."

Carter's tally was so long that its head popped above the water when my wife began to gently stroke it. I could see the delight in her eyes as she watched loads of pre-cum pouring into the pool out of his tool's thick head.

"Why don't you put that snake into my wife's mouth?" I asked.

"Can I do that to you, Jeni?"

"Yes, please do."

Carter then stood up while Jeni moved her head towards his rock-hard cock. Soon his prick was seven inches into Jeni's throat.

"Wow, Carter—you're still only halfway down," I muttered under my breath.

By then, my wife was bobbing her head up and down his shaft, trying desperately to get it as far down her throat as she could while massaging his grapefruit-sized balls. At the same time, he was squeezing her tits—one in each hand.

"I'm gonna come in your wife's mouth now, Bill," groaned the black man as he twitched and shot load after load of hot sperm down Jeni's throat. She swallowed every last drop.

"That was sweet and salty at the same time—simply delicious, Carter—thank you! Do you feel better now?"

"Yes, and my depression has pretty well disappeared."

"Is there anything else we can do for you today, Carter?" I asked.

"Just one more thing, Mr. Talbot."

"What would that be?"
"I'd like to make love to your wife."

"Jeni, are you up for that?"

"Why not—let's go all the way today," she replied.

I encouraged Jeni and Carter to get out of the tub, dry off and go inside to our master bedroom.

"Lie down sideways, Jeni, so your head tilts parallel to the bed and put your ass on that red cushion."

When she obeyed without hesitation, her feet stuck out over the far side of our bed, and her thick, black mound of pubic hair beckoned. At the same time, her vagina was in a raised position and wide open. I then began massaging her shoulders and bare breasts to get her into the mood for love.

"You can make love to me now, Carter, but please be gentle and go slow--your member is like a tree trunk," sighed Jeni, hot with anticipation and desire.

The black man was able to get his prick halfway into Jeni's body as she writhed in pleasure and sheer delight.

"Bill, I'm stretched to the limit but don't make him stop. Let him ravage me."

"Fuck her hard now, Carter," I urged, continuing to rub my wife's tits while she was watching a jet black diesel splitting her in half. "Put your hands on his ass and pull him in hard," I added. "And while you do that, I'm gonna put my cock in your mouth so open wide."

I wish I'd been able to video that scene because it was very erotic and I was extremely aroused. As a strange black man fucked my wife, she gave me a masterful blow job, taking my soaking wet penis hard and right down to the balls.

"Let's both come at the same time, Carter—okay."

"It better be soon, Bill."

A short time later, both of us exploded into Jeni's body. She got another injection of Carter's sperm—this time splashing up against her womb and filling her feminine cavity completely and another litre of liquid down her throat, from me.

"Swallow it all, Dear, just like you did for Carter," I screamed.

"I will. Darling. I will," she promised.

In the aftermath, we were all bathed in an atmosphere of love and acceptance. We lay together on our multi-coloured Persian eiderdown for over an hour before dressing.

Later that day, I asked Jeni how she liked our sexual adventure.

"Our lovemaking was a real gift to Carter, Bill. We took him from a depression to a state of pure ecstasy," she affirmed.

"Shall we invite him over again then?" I asked.

"Yes, of course."

About the Author

K. Tarumi is a resident of Northern British Columbia who writes books intending to help people heal their inner wounds and experience liberation from fear, anxiety, and depression. These works are based on three deeply held convictions: The whole realm of sexuality is ripe for revealing beauty in all its aspects; Romantic love is a mystery even with all its passions and conflicts; And life's sacredness can be experienced in each moment of passionate, sensual experiences between authentic and intentional people.